P9-CBC-780

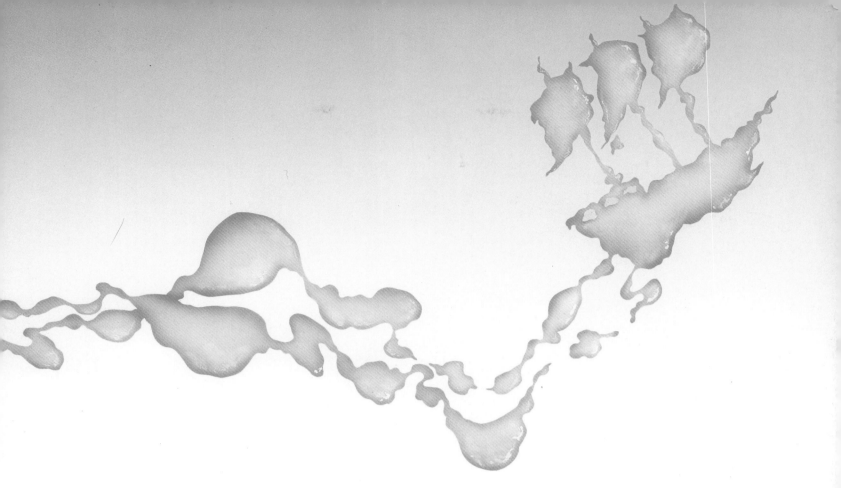

"Uncle Walter, are my parents coming back soon?"
Lila asked hopefully.

"In a few days, Lila. Don't worry, we'll have plenty of
fun."

Lila wilted. Fun with old Uncle Walter seemed about
as likely as a trip to the moon.

"You know, Lila," Uncle Walter chuckled, "I once had
to spend a summer with my Great Aunt Hortensia."

"A whole summer? Weren't you bored?"

"At first I was, but that was before I discovered the
secret of Old Zeb…"

"The what of who?" blinked Lila.

To
Kenny Klusmier and his cellar of wonders
where Katie, Erin, and Lauren were always welcome.
Miss Loretta Tindall's fifth grade class of splendid editors.
Julie and Sonni Strickland
Linda and James Garner
My three remarkable daughters, Katie, Erin, and Lauren,
may all your ships come in —CAD

To
my mother, MaryLee White, who gave me
the encouragement and direction to follow my dreams.
Special thanks to my wife Traci for her patience and support of this book
and to my fathers-in-law, Michael A. Graziano and Phillip E. Parker,
for their support of my artwork. —MPW

This Book Belongs To

_ _ _ _ _ _ _ _ _ _ _ _ _ _ _ _ is my love. My life.

Published by
Peachtree Publishers, Ltd.
1700 Chattahoochee Avenue
Atlanta, Georgia 30318-2112

www.peachtree-online.com

Text © 1997 by Carmen Agra Deedy
Illustrations © 1997 by Michael P. White

All rights reserved. No part of this publication may be reproduced, stored in a retrieval system, or
transmitted in any form or by any means—electronic, mechanical, photocopy, recording, or any
other—except for brief quotations in printed reviews, without the prior written permission of the Publisher.

Book design and composition by Loraine M. Joyner

Manufactured in December 2009 by Imago in Singapore

10 9 8 7 6 (hardcover)
10 9 8 7 6 5 (trade paperback)

Library of Congress Cataloging-in-Publication Data
Deedy, Carmen Agra.
    The secret of Old Zeb / Carmen Agra Deedy ; illustrated by Michael P. White. —1st ed.
        p. cm.
    Summary: Disappointed when his parents go off to climb Mount Kilimanjaro and leave him
        behind with his Great Aunt Hortensia, young Walter encounters mystery and intrigue when he
        meets Old Zeb, a shipbuilder with a secret dream.
            ISBN 13: 978-1-56145-115-9 / ISBN 10: 1-56145-115-0 (hardcover)
            ISBN 13: 978-1-56145-280-4 / ISBN 10: 1-56145-280-7 (trade paperback)
            [1. Shipbuilding—Fiction. 2. Great-aunts—Fiction.] I. White, Michael P., ill. II. Title.
        PZ7.D3587Se 1997
        [Fic]—dc21   97-12346
                                                               CIP
                                                               AC

THE SECRET OF

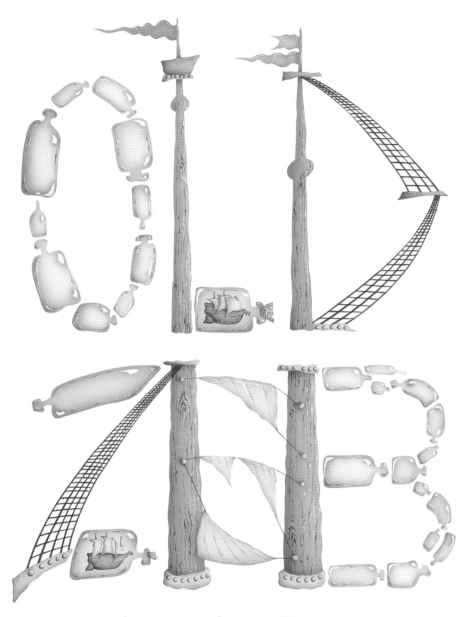

OLD ZEB

CARMEN AGRA DEEDY

ILLUSTRATED BY MICHAEL P. WHITE

PEACHTREE

ATLANTA

Mount Kilimanjaro, Tanzania ✠

Portrait of me, Walter
(I'm little, but I'm scrappy)

What's the difference
between a pith helmet
and me?—The pith helmet
gets to go to Africa

My favorite socks—day
seven of captivity

Steamer trunk—
roomy enough for
two parents?
(I'll take the
first-class cabin)

I AM LEFT BEHIND

I felt lost that summer. Really lost.

My parents had joined another expedition, this time to climb Mount Kilimanjaro.

As usual, they would leave me behind.

"You are to stay in Boston with Great Aunt Hortensia. You're going to have a wonderful summer, Walter," my mother cooed sweetly as she tried on her pith helmet before the parlor mirror.

"Aunt *who?*"

"Just remember Walter—no tomfoolery." My father grinned, inspecting a map of Africa.

"What about **Walter**foolery?" I quipped.

But Father, busy tracing the road to Tanzania, hadn't heard me.

One day, I felt sure, they were going to figure out what a funny kid they kept leaving behind.

Drowning in self-pity, I sat on a steamer trunk and tried to imagine life with a great aunt named Hortensia—me, Walter, chained to her card table, playing hours of canasta, polishing mountains of silver, and wearing lilac water in my hair.

CHAPTER TWO

I Go to Boston and My Adventure Begins

I was right about everything but the chains.

Aunt Hortensia was a no-nonsense Victorian and I grew to hate canasta.

So I hid out in my room whenever possible to read my astronomy books and stargaze. From my window at 121 East Longfellow, I had a clear view of Boston Harbor. I would watch the tall ships longingly.

Oh, to be a stowaway aboard one of them—destination Tanzania. But how?

As if in answer, one night a grizzled old sailor appeared through the mist. It looked as if King Neptune had walked right out of the sea.

Excitedly, I watched him climb the steps that led…next door!

He squinted one eye toward my window and I stepped back.

Who was he? *What* was he?

My eyes fell on the sack he carried. Was he a smuggler, perhaps? He might be just the fellow to help a stowaway reach his parents.

I decided to keep watch on the brownstone at 122 East Longfellow.

My prison cell at 121 East Longfellow

One night a grizzled old sailor
appeared through the mist.

CHAPTER THREE

IN WHICH MY HOPES ARE DASHED AND MY HEAD IS DOUSED

My suspicions grew daily.

Next door, swarthy sailors came and went, lugging sea chests and crates from the dock.

One afternoon, I shared my theory about our neighbor with Aunt Hortensia as she doused my head with lilac water.

"A *smuggler*? Walter, what an imagination! That is Old Zeb. He's just a lonely old fellow who makes ships in bottles."

"But what about all the packages?" I persisted.

"He is probably…*redecorating.*"

With that one word, my hopes sank.

"Well, whatever he is," I rallied, "I'll bet he doesn't put perfume in his hair!"

"*Cologne,* Walter—"

I'd stopped listening. I saw that a fresh crate was arriving at our neighbor's doorstep. I excused myself and ran outside to investigate.

I was just prying the lid open a crack when a voice above me thundered, "Hello, boy! Are you lost?"

I felt a drop of excitement in an ocean of dread as I backed up and looked into the face of Old Zeb.

"Hello, boy! Are you lost?"

CHAPTER FOUR

TRAPPED BETWEEN THE SCOURGE OF THE SEVEN SEAS AND THE TERROR OF THE DEEP

I was right about everything but the smuggling.

The old tar was a pirate.

Pirate. Pirate. Pirate.

Right out of my picturebooks. As real as Captain Bligh, Old Peg Leg, or Bluebeard himself! Why, I'd bet scores of kids disappeared into his cellar.

"I asked if you were lost!" Old Zeb snorted and hammered the floor with his cane.

"No, sir," I squeaked.

"Great Guns!" he roared. "What skullduggery have we here?"

Rats! Old Zeb had seen the crack in the crate. So much for my stowaway scheme.

He moved toward me and I bolted, flying over the cobblestones in an air-sucking, arm-pumping run.

Breathless, I turned down the first alleyway behind our row of brownstones and stopped cold. Before me loomed the inky shadow of a monstrous sea serpent.

Then I turned my head to look behind me and the sight I saw made the hairs on my neck stand on end…

Before me loomed…a monstrous sea serpent.

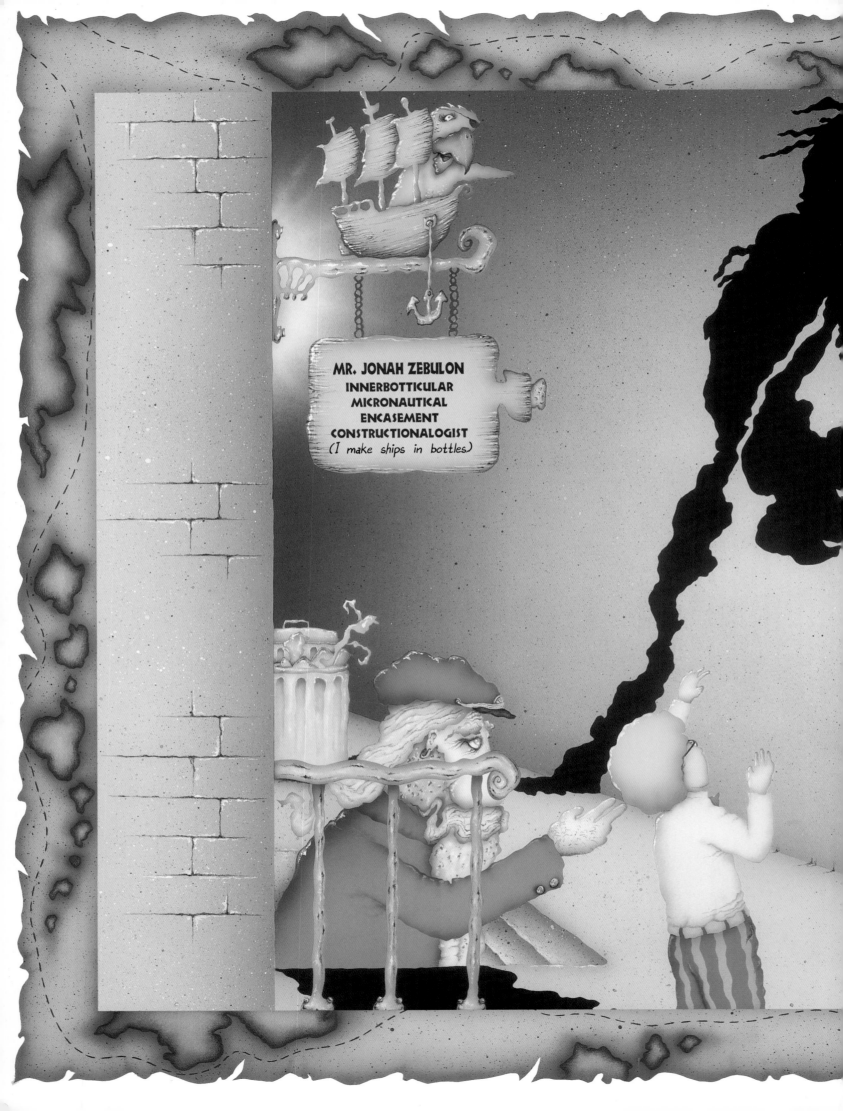

CHAPTER FIVE

CAPTURED!

It was the old buccaneer again.

"Still lost, boy?"

I pointed a shaky finger at the shadow on the brick wall.

"Holy mackerel, son! *Face your monster, not his shadow,*" he growled as he spun me around. I gasped: my Terror of the Deep was…an overflowing trash bin.

"Very brave," he congratulated me. "Monsters always turn to rubbish when you look them in the eye."

"But it wasn't a monster. My imagination just took sail again. Why, I was convinced *you* were a *pirate!*" I confessed.

He laughed (a little too heartily, I thought).

Abruptly he asked, "May I show you something?"

All my suspicions returned.

"Not your cellar, I hope?" I asked nervously, taking a step back.

His good eye narrowed as he whispered, "And how do you know about my *cellar*?"

CHAPTER SIX

A Mystery Is Revealed

I cautiously followed Old Zeb into his house. It was just like a maritime museum. One glorious treasure—an ancient gold compass—caught my eye.

"Too bad you don't have a ship to mount it on," I hinted.

"Who says I don't?" he answered gruffly.

Things were looking better by the minute.

Then he handed me a small sea-green bottle. Trapped inside was a miniature Spanish galleon.

"No, I mean a *real* ship."

He ignored me and blustered on, "Let me show you how to build a ship in a bottle." Gingerly, he unfurled a diagram and the mystery was revealed.

"So that's how it's done," I whispered.

"Ships are my love. My life. And I've got one that'll really put the wind in your sails," boasted Old Zeb.

"First," I said, "I want to see you squeeze that huge compass into this little bottle."

But there was no answer.

He was gone.

The magnificent compass—object of my obsession.

Then he handed me a small sea-green bottle.

CHAPTER SEVEN

THE OLD SEA DOG VANISHES

"Zeb?" I called out softly.

No answer.

He's probably gone down to the cellar, I reassured myself.

The *cellar*?

A chill went up my spine and my imagination went **BERSERK**—I could almost see the piles of kid-bones. Sure, first it's the old ship-in-the-bottle routine, then he lowers the boom and you're ballast for his pirate ship!

Just a lonely old fellow, eh? Aunt Hortensia was sure out to sea on this one.

But *I* was onto him. Or was I wrong again? (I remembered the Embarrassing Sea-Serpent Incident.)

"Old Zeb!" I called once more.

Still no answer.

I stepped into the hallway and felt a crunching on the dark wooden planks under my feet.

A trail of sawdust and wood shavings led me to a door framed with a thread of light. At that moment, I completely forgot my plan to join my parents on their adventure.

I had found the c
e
l
l
a
r
.

The shavings led me to a door
framed with a thread of light.

CHAPTER EIGHT

I Discover the G.S.P.

I'd been wrong about *everything*.

Old Zeb's secret was...an enormous ship.

Built right under our noses—right under boring East Longfellow. *Right under old Aunt Hortensia.*

"Ahoy!" Old Zeb waved from the stern.

I stared, slackjawed, at the biggest vessel I'd ever seen. "It's STUPENDOUS."

"Aye, Walter!" he shouted. "Some dreams are too big to be kept in bottles."

"Does she have a name?"

"I call her the Milky Way, because she's the nearest thing to heaven I know."

I had to agree.

"But I'm getting old," his voice echoed, "and she's still not finished."

"Could I help?" I called out eagerly.

His smile was my answer. (You'd think he'd planned it this way all along.)

We worked that afternoon and when it was time for me to go, Old Zeb whispered, "Now, mum's the word about this G.S.P."

"G.S.P.?" I piped.

"Great Secret Project," he cautioned. "There'll be no slipups if we stick to a code name."

The old tar was a genius.

Now to face Hortensia, the Warden.

CHAPTER NINE

IN WHICH I TELL AUNT HORTENSIA
A DELIBERATE FALSEHOOD

"Walter, you tell me immediately where you have been all day!"

Time to walk the plank.

"Next door. W-w-with Old Zeb."

The truth caught her off guard.

"Doing what?" she asked, her eyes narrowing.

"...redecorating?" I ventured.

"Walter Everest Higgins! That is a deliberate falsehood."

"I c-c-can't tell you. I promised," I whimpered as I draped myself limply over the arm of the divan.

"Walter, theatrics will not work with me."

"I can't tell you about the G.S.P.," I whined.

"Now we're getting somewhere. G.S.P., eh? Well, I'm your G.A.H.—Great Aunt Hortensia— and I say you can. Unless you wish to spend the rest of the summer polishing silver."

"I don't care! It's Old Zeb's dream and he needs my help! How could you understand? I'll bet you've never had a dream in your life!"

UH-OH.

Aunt Hortensia's back stiffened and a whalebone in her corset snapped.

"So I've never had a dream, Walter? Had 'em and lived 'em. Sit up, pardner."

Pardner?

I whimpered as I draped myself
limply over the arm of the divan.

CHAPTER TEN

BOOTS AND SPURS

Aunt Hortensia—a silver miner?

My head reeled as she spoke dreamily of running away to Colorado during the Silver Rush of 1878.

Did every grown-up I know have a secret life?

"Wait," I interrupted, "—you ran away?"

"Well, there are two kinds of running away, Walter: running away *from* and running away *to*. I had to go. The call of the West was too strong. It was my love. My life."

Where had I heard those words before?

I tried to picture Aunt Hortensia happily grubstaking with the miners.

"I'm sorry, Aunt Hortensia. I just can't imagine you in anything but satin and lace."

And that's how I came to own her boots and spurs.

When I climbed into bed, Aunt Hortensia came to say good night.

"My parents love climbing mountains the way you loved the West and Old Zeb loves his ships," I said.

"And they love you, Walter," she added.

"But they left *me, Walter*, behind," I pointed out.

"They'll come back, dear." She kissed my cheek. "Meanwhile, you should climb your own Kilimanjaro."

I closed my eyes and saw the Milky Way.

Aunt Hortensia—a silver miner?

"Nice boots, Walter," Old Zeb
remarked drily.

IN WHICH I CLIMB
THE MILKY WAY

I reported for G.S.P. duty the next morning.

"Nice boots, Walter," Old Zeb remarked drily.

It turned out that Zeb knew all about Aunt Hortensia's prospecting days.

"Your Aunt Hortie's one of the lucky ones, Walter. She's lived her dream…I'm still building mine," he sighed.

"We'll get it done, Old Zeb." I tried to sound cheerful. "Before you know it we'll be mounting the compass."

He shook his head. "Won't be mounting any compass where I'm going. I know the way."

"Where *are* we going?" I asked.

He gave me an odd look. "*We?* This is my journey, son. You won't feel so lost when you follow your own dream."

"Well, *you'll* be lost without a compass," I said stubbornly.

"We all have a compass inside, Walter." He watched me carefully. "It's the part of us that points to what's right and sure and *true*."

"Will it point me to my dream?"

Old Zeb nodded.

"Like true north on a compass."

CHAPTER TWELVE

WE CALL ON THE SAILMAKER
WITH PIECES OF EIGHT

A few weeks later, we called on a surly sailmaker.

"Well, Old Zeb," he smirked, "more linen scraps for your tiny ships?"

"Aye," Old Zeb nodded. "Six hundred fifty-six yards, to be exact."

That took the wind out of his sails.

"But I can't possibly—"

"How unfortunate," lamented Old Zeb. "We'll have to take our money elsewhere."

"Wait!" cried the shopkeeper, not about to lose the biggest sail of his life. "I'll need the money up front."

With a grin, Old Zeb offered a handful of gold doubloons and said, "Come, Walter."

"You should have told him about the G.S.P.," I whispered excitedly as we stepped outside.

Old Zeb turned to me sharply.

"Walter, if a man belittles your work, he's certainly not going to think much of your dreams."

"We'll have the last laugh," I insisted. "Just wait till we put to sea." (I stressed the "we.")

"To sea? Whatever made you think the Milky Way was going to be put to *sea*?"

Ka-ching, ka-ching!

I found him snoring, asleep at his desk.

CHAPTER THIRTEEN

TIME IS RUNNING OUT

All summer we worked on the ship.

Packages came from exotic ports—Sydney, Istanbul, Havana. Finally the *last* delivery arrived.

"Zeb! It's the anchor!"

I found him snoring, asleep at his desk. I shook him gently.

"Walter?" he mumbled drowsily.

"Come on, Zeb, the anchor's here," I repeated.

"I heard you, Walter, but this bottled schooner is due to the harbormaster's today."

"Forget these little toy boats," I snapped. "We have a dream to build, remember?"

Old Zeb eyed me slowly. "Well, that was quite a gale, Walter. Dreams don't build themselves. Ever stopped to think how many bottled ships I've had to make to build the Milky Way?"

My stars.

I gulped and handed him a tiny mast.

We worked quietly side by side till evening. When I left to deliver the schooner to the harbormaster, Old Zeb was sleeping peacefully and the Milky Way was ready to sail.

CHAPTER FOURTEEN

WHAT I HEARD FROM MY WINDOW

At home, I said good night and left Aunt Hortensia happily playing canasta with her friends. Upstairs, I could still hear their voices through the open window.

"It's really very sad about Old Mr. Zebulon, Hortie."

"Sad?" Aunt Hortensia asked.

"Oh yes. They're saying in town that he's gone quite daft. Loo-loo. Only one oar in the water."

"Nonsense!" Aunt Hortensia shot back. "Why, he's done wonders for Walter. He's a perfectly respectable gentleman, too. And I *dare* anyone at this table to say differently."

("You tell 'em Aunt Hortie," I cheered.)

"Well, he's making a fool of himself down at the harbor. The sailmaker says he's bought a thousand yards of sailcloth. Imagine! For those little ships. *And* he's written his sister about some great secret…" continued one of the women.

I listened hard, gripping the windowsill.

"If you ask me, she's coming to take him home with her to Iowa *just in time.*"

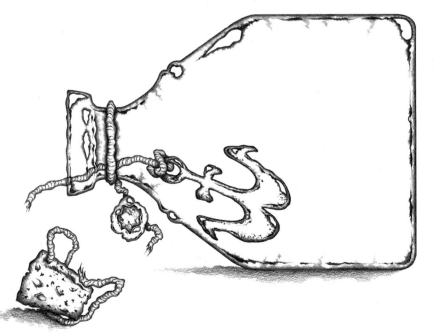

Oh no! I had to warn him.

I slipped outside and ran into Old Zeb's shop. His chair was empty.

The cellar!

I ran and pulled open the door…

The ship was gone.

I ran and pulled open the door...

CHAPTER FIFTEEN

I Find My Way

Left behind.

Once again, I felt lost.

I turned a heavy foot toward home. Outside the door I stumbled over another blasted package—it was addressed to me. I tore at the paper.

Inside was Old Zeb's compass. I thought I would cry as I read his smudged and wrinkled note.

Dear Walter,
I'm sorry I can't take you on my final journey. No time for teary goodbyes—I have to fly.
And as for you—it's high time you followed your own dreams. You won't need this compass, son. You've known the way all along. Use it as a paperweight!
Ever true north,
Old Zeb

Gone. Old Zeb and the Milky Way. How could it be?

The harbor! Maybe I'll find them there.

I raced down the alleyway and onto the docks. My eyes scanned the merchant ships.

"Walter!"

I rubbed my eyes. Was I dreaming? There were my *parents* standing on the dock by their steamer trunk.

"We're back early, Walter," my father beamed. "We remembered what a funny kid we'd left behind."

For once, I had no snappy comeback. You see, I was speechless the moment my eyes caught sight of the Milky Way.

My crusty old friend had kept his very best secret even from me...

Inside was Old Zeb's compass.

...the Milky Way
was never meant to sail.

She was made to fly.

Lila sighed, "Uncle Walter, that's awesome! But did you ever climb Mount Kilimanjaro?"

"No, no, dear. That was my parents' dream."

"What was *your* dream?"

"Haven't you guessed? The stars, Lila. The boundless, uncharted universe. It's always been my love. My life."

"Huh?"

"Lila, dear, how would you like to pay a visit to my attic?"

WORDS
OLD ZEB
WOULD KNOW

BALLAST—Stones or lead or other heavy material placed in the ship's hold (cargo deck) to help keep it upright and stable.

BUCCANEER—Pirate. Also called sea rover, robber, sea king, privateer.

COMPASS—Device used for determining direction which consists of a magnetized needle that turns on a pivot and points north.

GALLEON—Sailing ship used for trading by the Spaniards and a favorite target of English privateers.

SCHOONER—Sailing ship developed in the United States in the early 1700s and used for fishing.

STERN—Rear section of a ship. The front section of a ship is called the bow.

STOWAWAY—Person who hides aboard a ship to obtain free transportation.

TAR—Sailor. Other names are mariner, old salt, seadog, seafarer.